Goodnight
Beautiful
Moon

Come and play
on the little island of
Puffin Rock!

This is **Oona**. And this is **Baba**!

Otto is Oona and Baba's friend in the sky. He knows everything about everything!

SEAGULL CLIFF

PUFFIN BURROWS

MEADOW

MAY'S BURROW

FLYNNE'S LAIR

HOOTS' STUMP

MOSSY'S DEN

May is a fun-loving bunny rabbit. Bouncy and chatty, she is always ready for an adventure!

DEEP SEA

BERNIE'S GROTTO

DUNES

ROCK O' CRABS

Silky is a gentle and loving seal with an infectious laugh. She lives in the sea with her mum.

SEAL'S SAND BANK

CORAL REEF

It's a bright and sunny afternoon on Puffin Rock and everyone is enjoying the sunshine – even Otto! Otto's an owl, so usually he spends the day asleep in his nest.

Squaaawk!

Not today, though.

"I'm too **excited** to sleep!" he cries.

Baba
boo!

Otto flaps his wings and hoots excitedly.
"Tonight's the night, Oona!
There's going to be a
supermoon!"

"What's a **supermoon**,
Otto?" asks Oona.

"The moon is super close to us – so it'll be super big!
It'll light up the **whole island!**"

HOₒₒₒt!

"Wow, Otto!" Oona gasps.
"I can't wait to see it!"

Otto blinks sleepily. "I think I'll go and have a nap before **moonrise,**" he says, flapping into the air. "I'll come back here to the burrow to find you when it's time!"

Yaaaawn

Little Baba gives a big yawn – but Oona is much too **excited** to sleep.

"You go and have a nap too, Baba," she says.
"I'm going to stay up and tell
everyone about the **moon!**"

As she runs off, Oona bumps into her friend.

Bump!

"Hello, Mossy! Have you heard
about the **supermoon** tonight?"

"A supermoon?" asks Mossy. "Where?"

But Oona is already running on.

"Meet us at the burrow at moonrise!" she calls back.
"I'm going to tell May!"

Oona runs as fast as her legs can carry her. By the time she finds May in the meadow, she is completely out of breath.

"May! May! Tonight! Moon! Big! Round! Meet us at the burrow at moonrise!"

"Slow down, Oona," says May, laughing. "What did you say about the moon?"

Quickly, Oona explains.

But before she has got her breath back she's on her way again,
desperate to find Silky to tell her about the moon too.

The sun is beginning to set as Oona slides
down a sand dune towards Silky.

Silky is unsure. "I'd love to see it,"
she says, "but I don't usually
stay up late . . ."

Wheeeee!

Oona's eyelids are getting
heavier and **heavier** . . .

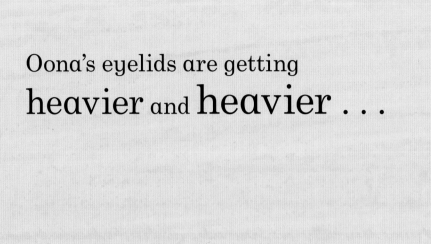

Her head is **dropping** . . .
And in **no** time at all . . .

. . . Oona is **fast asleep!**

zZzzZ

Otto arrives at the puffin burrows with his
brother and sister but there's no sign of Oona.
Papa seems **worried**.

Otto flutters up and down anxiously. "Where's Oona?" he asks. "We agreed to meet here to go and see the moon!"

HOᵒᵒot!

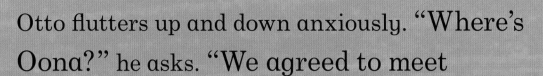

"She hasn't come home yet," says Papa. "Has anyone seen her?"

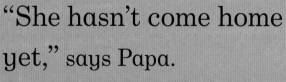

"Last time I saw Oona, she was going to see **May**," says Mossy.

But Oona isn't in the **meadow**.

"Last time I saw Oona," says May,
"she was going to see Silky!"

So together they rush to the beach.

Silky is snoozing on the sand but wakes up with a start.

"Is the moon here?" she cries.

"Not yet, Silky," says Papa. "We're looking for Oona.
Have you seen her?"

But, before Silky can answer, they hear
a frantic **hooting**.

Hoot!

Hooooooot!

Hoot!

zzzzZ

"Here she is!" calls Otto, as
Papa lands beside him, laughing with
relief to see Oona safe and sound.

May sighs softly. "Poor Oona," she says.
"She SO wanted to see the moon.
She must have tired herself out!"

Papa calls gently to Oona to wake her up, but when her eyes open she flaps into the air.

"The moon! The supermoon! Oh no, I've missed it!" she cries.

"No, Oona," says Otto. "Look!"

Together, they turn to gaze
up at the sky, and see . . .

. . . the moon.

Oona and her friends stay up late into the night, while Puffin Rock is bathed in silver moonlight.
"Goodnight, beautiful moon," whispers Oona.

The End